Two Terrible Frights

To the Westview Library,
with love!

'93

To Jeri and Norm, with love!   (J.A.)
For the littlest mouse and L.B.   (E.C.)

Two Terrible Frights

by Jim Aylesworth

illustrated by Eileen Christelow

Atheneum   New York

ONCE UPON A TIME, there was
a big old farm house, way out in the country.

Downstairs, in the basement, in a cozy corner, a little mouse was thinking about a bedtime snack.

And upstairs, in a cozy room, a little girl was also thinking about a bedtime snack.

The little mouse went to her mother and said, "Mommy, can I have a snack before I go to bed? Maybe a little piece of cheese?" The little mouse's mother said, "Yes, but you'll have to go up to the kitchen and get it for yourself. I've been working all day, and I'm tired."

And at just about the very same moment, the little girl
went to her mother and said, "Mommy, can I have a snack
before I go to bed? Maybe a little glass of milk?" The
little girl's mother said, "Yes, but you'll have to go
down to the kitchen and get it for yourself. I've been
at work all day, and I'm tired."

The little mouse said, "I can't go up there all by myself! There might be a monster or something just waiting to get me!" The little mouse's mother said, "Don't be silly."

The little girl said, "I can't go down there all by myself! There
might be a creature or something that'll jump out and get me!"
The little girl's mother said, "How ridiculous."

So, the little mouse started for the kitchen,
all by herself,
. . . quietly up the radiator pipe,
. . . tiptoe under the floor . . .

. . . through a dark hole,

. . . under the stove,

. . . and out across the kitchen floor.

And at just about the very same moment, the little girl
also started for the kitchen, all by herself,
. . . quietly down the long hall,
. . . tiptoe down the stairs . . .

. . . through the dark parlor,
. . . through the dining room,
. . . and into the kitchen.

And just when the little mouse was right in the middle of the floor, the little girl flipped on the light.

CLICK

They both stood very very still, and looked at each other.

Then, at just about the very same moment, the little mouse went "SQUEAK!", and the little girl went "EEEK!", and they both took off running!

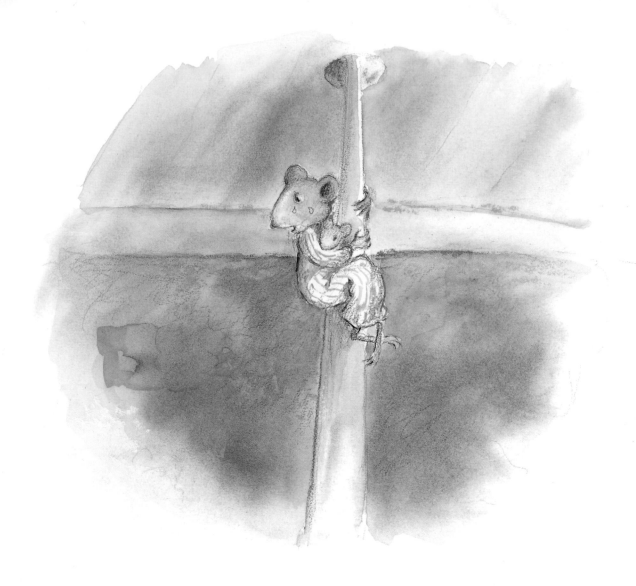

The little mouse ran back under the stove, back down the hole, back under the floor, back down the radiator pipe, all the while hollering, "Mommy! Mommy! Mommy!"

And just as fast, the little girl ran back through the dining room, back through the parlor, back up the stairs, back down the hallway, all the while hollering, "Mommy! Mommy! Mommy!"

The little mouse sobbed, "There was a person up there, and it 'eeeked' at me."

The little girl sobbed, "There was a mouse down there, and it 'squeaked' at me."

"Now, now, now," said the little mouse's mother. "I can tell that you've had a terrible fright, but I'll bet that person you saw was a little girl person, and you probably scared her worse than she scared you."

"Now, now, now," said the little girl's mother. "I can tell that you've had a terrible fright, but I'll just bet that mouse you saw was a little girl mouse, and you probably scared her worse than she scared you."

"Do you really think so?" said the little mouse, drying her tears and crawling into bed. "I hope I didn't scare her too bad." "I'm sure she'll get over it," said the little mouse's mother. Then she kissed her on the cheek and said goodnight.

"Do you really think so?" said the little girl, drying her tears and crawling into bed. "I hope I didn't scare her too bad." "I'm sure she'll get over it," said the little girl's mother. Then, she kissed her on the cheek and said goodnight.

The little mouse fell asleep in her soft bed, thinking about the little girl.

And at just about the very same moment, the little girl fell
asleep in her soft bed, thinking about the little mouse.

And they both dreamed . . .

. . . about **each** other.

Atheneum
Macmillan Publishing Company
866 Third Avenue, New York, NY 10022

Type set by V & M Graphics, New York City
Printed and bound by Toppan Printing Company, Japan
Typography by Mary Ahern
First Edition

10 9 8 7 6 5 4 3 2

Library of Congress Cataloging-in-Publication Data

Aylesworth, Jim.   Two terrible frights.

SUMMARY: A little girl mouse and a little girl person meet while getting a snack in the kitchen at bedtime and scare each other—only to dream of each other later.
[1. Bedtime—Fiction. 2. Mice—Fiction] I. Christelow, Eileen, ill. II. Title.
PZ7.A983Tw   1987   [E]   86-25859
ISBN 0-689-31327-6